Professional Crocodile

BY GIOVANNA ZOBOLI & MARIACHIARA DI GIORGIO

chronicle books
san francisco

First published in the United States of America in 2017 by Chronicle Books LLC.

Originally published in Italy in 2017 under the title *Profressione coccodrillo* by Topipittori, Viale Isonzo, 16, 20135 Milan, Italy.

Copyright © 2017 by Topipittori.

Library of Congress Cataloging-in-Publication Data available.

ISBN 978-1-4521-6506-6

Manufactured in Italy.

Jacket design by Alice Seiler.

10 9 8 7 6 5 4 3 2 1

Chronicle Books LLC
680 Second Street
San Francisco, California 94107
www.chroniclekids.com

DR/////INN

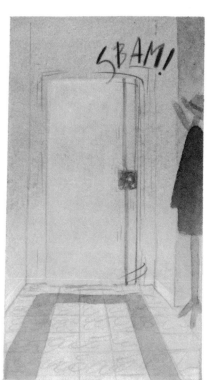